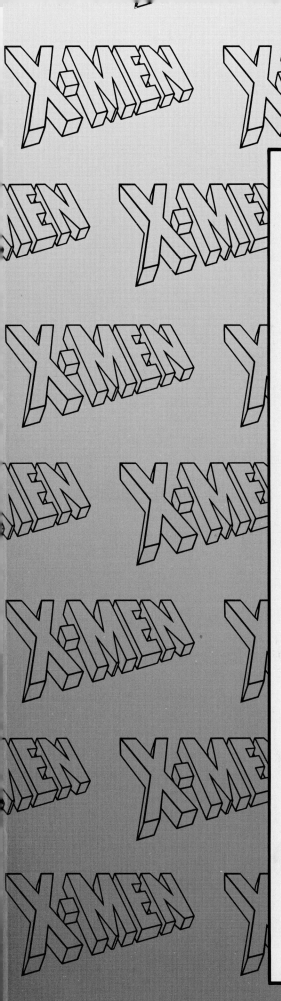
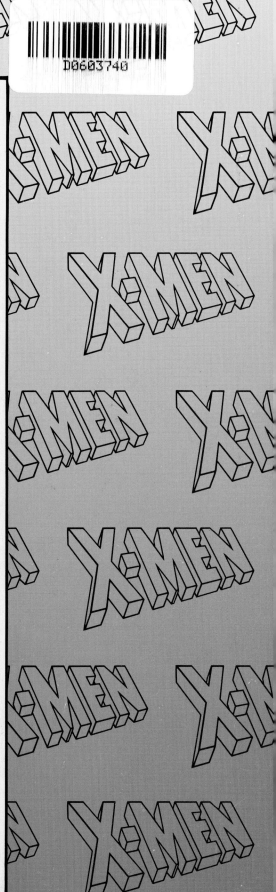

LOOK & FIND

X-MEN

Danger Room • Genosha

Shi'ar Galaxy • Sentinels' Base

The Savage Land • and more!

Illustrator/Illustration Coordinator: James Janes
Inker: Dave Simons
Colorists: Janice Parker; Michele Marrero-DeCicco

Illustration Script Development by Dwight Zimmerman

Louis Weber, C.E.O.
Publications International, Ltd.
7373 N. Cicero Avenue
Lincolnwood, Illinois 60646

Manufactured in U.S.A.

8 7 6 5 4 3 2 1

ISBN 1-56173-703-8

PUBLICATIONS INTERNATIONAL, LTD.

I'VE NEVER SEEN SUCH CHAOS IN THE DANGER ROOM. FIRST MAGNETO BURST IN WITH HIS MINDMASTER DEVICE, PLANNING TO ENSLAVE THE X-MEN! JUST WHEN IT SEEMED HE MIGHT SUCCEED, GATEWAY APPEARED AND USED HIS MUTANT ABILITIES TO CREATE A TORNADO THAT FRAGMENTED THE MINDMASTER DEVICE AND DISRUPTED THE FABRIC OF TIME! I SENSE THAT GATEWAY'S INTENTIONS ARE GOOD, BUT I STILL DON'T SEE WHAT HE HAS IN MIND.

HELP PROFESSOR XAVIER AND THE X-MEN MAKE SENSE OF THIS CONFUSION. BEGIN BY FINDING THE PIECES OF MAGNETO'S MINDMASTER DEVICE.

RADAR DISH

CONTROL PANEL

MAIN HOUSING UNIT

GYROSCOPE

TRIPOD

RADAR SCREEN

USING CEREBRO, PROFESSOR X IS SENDING THE INFORMATION THAT THE X-MEN NEED TO RETURN. CAN YOU FIND THE PACKAGES HE'S SENT IT IN?

BOX
COURIER'S POUCH
FAX MACHINE
LARGE ENVELOPE
MAILING TUBE
SCROLL

BRAVE THE DANGERS OF THE SAVAGE LAND AND FIND THESE ITEMS FOR THE X-MEN.

GENOSHAN RIFLE

NO MUTANTS SIGN

GYROSCOPE

GATEWAY'S TIME WARP

GENOSHAN HELMET

PIPELINE

SEE IF YOU CAN SPOT THE ITEMS THE X-MEN NEED TO
TAKE THE NEXT STEP IN THEIR BATTLE WITH MAGNETO.

MAGNETO'S
FLAG

ACOLYTE'S
HELMET

SINGLE SEAT
ROCKET
PLANE

FABIAN
CORTEZ

RADAR
DISH

GATE-
WAY'S
TIME
WARP

HELP THE X-MEN FIND THE ITEMS THEY NEED BEFORE THE SENTINEL ARMY IS ACTIVATED.

SHI'AR CRUISER

SHI'AR HELMET

JET PACK

BROOD WARRIOR

GATEWAY'S TIME WARP

CONTROL PANEL

MY FAVORITE LITTLE VACATION SPOT--THE SHI'AR GALAXY. YOU CAN ALWAYS FIND A GOOD FIGHT HERE, AND TODAY'S NO EXCEPTION. THE BROOD'S AT IT AGAIN, AND PRINCESS LILANDRA AND HER WARRIORS COULD USE OUR HELP. I DON'T MIND TAKIN' OUT A FEW SLEAZOIDS WHILE WE LOOK FOR GATEWAY'S TIME KEYS.

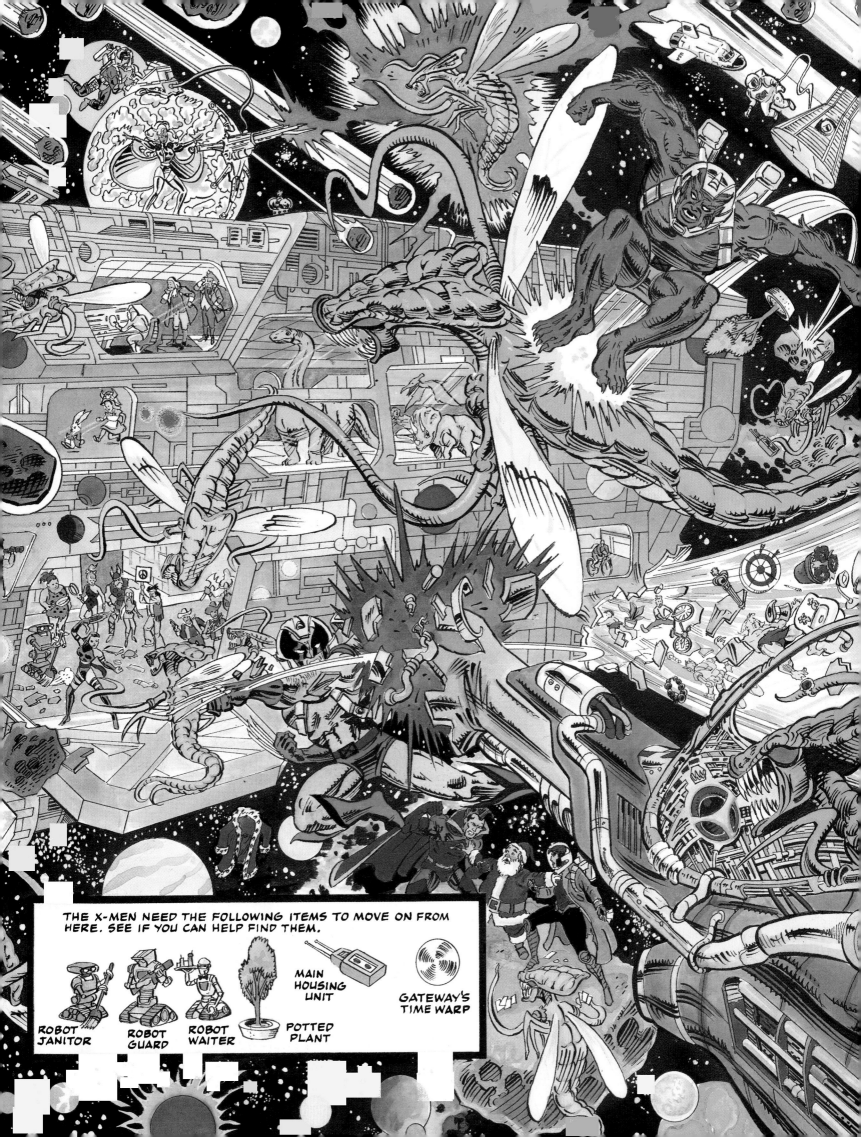

THE X-MEN NEED THE FOLLOWING ITEMS TO MOVE ON FROM HERE. SEE IF YOU CAN HELP FIND THEM.

ROBOT JANITOR

ROBOT GUARD

ROBOT WAITER

POTTED PLANT

MAIN HOUSING UNIT

GATEWAY'S TIME WARP

WHEN THE X-MEN ARE THROUGH, MAGNETO AND HIS MINIONS WILL BE NEEDING MEDICAL ATTENTION. SEE IF YOU CAN FIND THESE MEDICAL SUPPLIES FOR THEM.

WHEEL CHAIR

NEEDLE

FIRST AID KIT

DOCTOR

CRUTCHES

BANDAGES

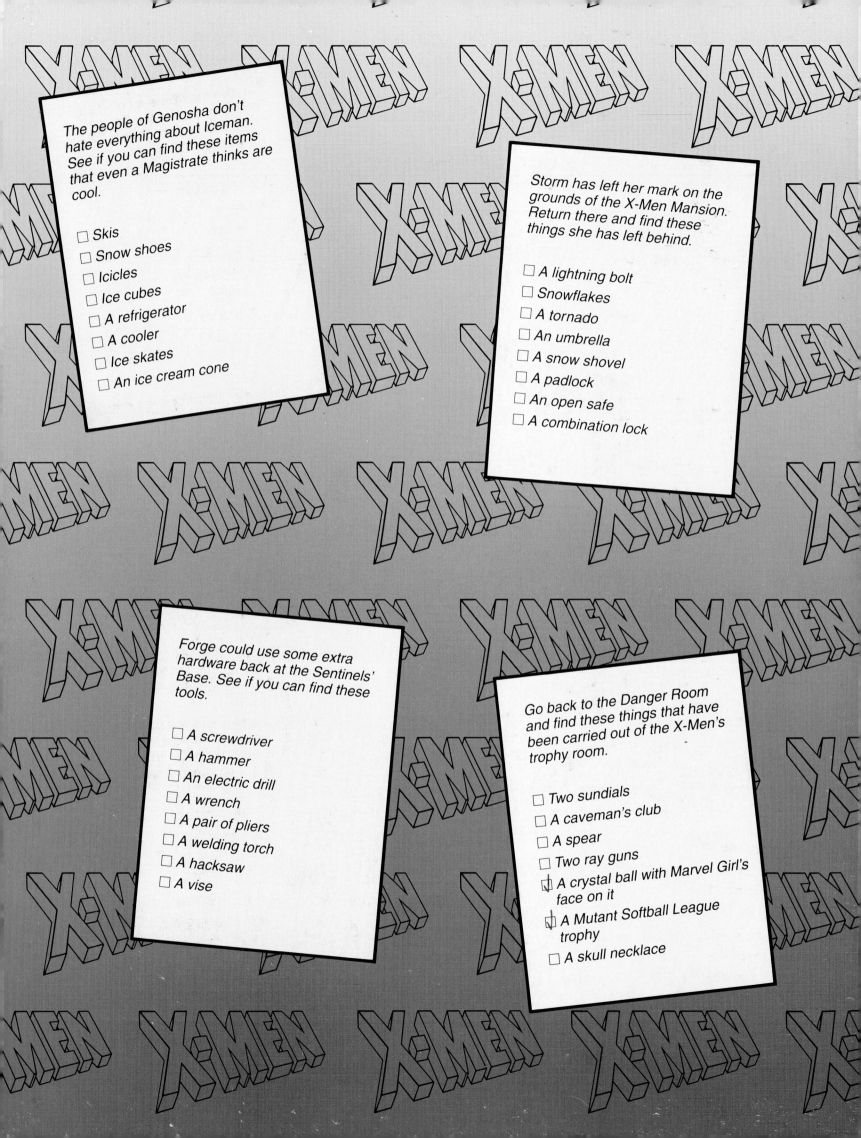

The people of Genosha don't hate everything about Iceman. See if you can find these items that even a Magistrate thinks are cool.

- ☐ Skis
- ☐ Snow shoes
- ☐ Icicles
- ☐ Ice cubes
- ☐ A refrigerator
- ☐ A cooler
- ☐ Ice skates
- ☐ An ice cream cone

Storm has left her mark on the grounds of the X-Men Mansion. Return there and find these things she has left behind.

- ☐ A lightning bolt
- ☐ Snowflakes
- ☐ A tornado
- ☐ An umbrella
- ☐ A snow shovel
- ☐ A padlock
- ☐ An open safe
- ☐ A combination lock

Forge could use some extra hardware back at the Sentinels' Base. See if you can find these tools.

- ☐ A screwdriver
- ☐ A hammer
- ☐ An electric drill
- ☐ A wrench
- ☐ A pair of pliers
- ☐ A welding torch
- ☐ A hacksaw
- ☐ A vise

Go back to the Danger Room and find these things that have been carried out of the X-Men's trophy room.

- ☐ Two sundials
- ☐ A caveman's club
- ☐ A spear
- ☐ Two ray guns
- ☑ A crystal ball with Marvel Girl's face on it
- ☑ A Mutant Softball League trophy
- ☐ A skull necklace